FREMONT PUBLIC LIBRARY

P9-BZS-250

A Beginning-to-Read Book

Dear Dragon's Colors 1,2,3

by Margaret Hillert

Illustrated by David Schimmell

WITHDRAWN

Fremont Public Library
1170 N. Midlothian Road
Mundelein, IL 60060

DEAR CAREGIVER, The *Beginning-to-Read* series is a carefully written collection of classic readers you may remember from your own childhood. Each book features text comprised of common sight words to provide your child ample practice reading the words that appear most frequently in written text. The many additional details in the pictures enhance the story and offer the opportunity for you to help your child expand oral language and develop comprehension.

Begin by reading the story to your child, followed by letting him or her read familiar words and soon your child will be able to read the story independently. At each step of the way, be sure to praise your reader's efforts to build his or her confidence as an independent reader. Discuss the pictures and encourage your child to make connections between the story and his or her own life. At the end of the story, you will find reading activities and a word list that will help your child practice and strengthen beginning reading skills.

Above all, the most important part of the reading experience is to have fun and enjoy it!

Shannon Cannon

Shannon Cannon,
Literacy Consultant

Norwood House Press • P.O. Box 316598 • Chicago, Illinois 60631
For more information about Norwood House Press please visit our website at
www.norwoodhousepress.com or call 866-565-2900.

Text copyright ©2011 by Margaret Hillert. Illustrations and cover design copyright ©2011 by Norwood House Press, Inc. All rights reserved. No part of this book may be reproduced or utilized in any form or by any means without written permission from the publisher.

LIBRARY OF CONGRESS CATALOGING-IN-PUBLICATION DATA
    Hillert, Margaret.
    Dear dragon's colors 1, 2, 3 / by Margaret Hillert ; illustrated by David
    Schimmell.
       p. cm.
    Summary: "A boy and his pet dragon have fun learning about counting and
    colors"--Provided by publisher.
     ISBN-13: 978-1-59953-376-6 (library edition : alk. paper)
    ISBN-10: 1-59953-376-6 (library edition : alk. paper)
    [1. Dragons--Fiction. 2. Color--Fiction. 3. Counting.] I. Schimmell, David
    ; ill. II. Title.
    PZ7.H558Dek 2010
    [E]--dc22
                                    2010007370
Manufactured in the United States of America in North Mankato, Minnesota.
                            280R—052015

Play with me.
Come play with me.
I like to play with cars.

1 little **red** car.
It can go, go, go.
It is fun to play with
a little **red** car.

1 little **red** car.

I have **2** little **blue** cars.
I can make them go up and
down.

2 little **blue** cars.

I have **3** little **yellow** cars.
Yellow cars are pretty.
They can go in and out.

3 little **yellow** cars.

I have **4** little **green** cars.
Green is good.
I like **green**.

4 little **green** cars.

I have **5** little **orange** cars.
Oh, oh, oh.
What is this?
This is not good.

5 little **orange** cars.

I have **6** little **brown** cars.
Go, cars. Go.
This is fun, fun, fun.

6 little **brown** cars.

I have **7** little **purple** cars.
Mother likes **purple**.
I like **purple**, too.

7 little **purple** cars.

I have **8** little **pink** cars.
How pretty.
Pink, pink, pink.

8 little **pink** cars.

I have **9** little **black** cars.
This is good.

9 little **black** cars.

I have **10** little **white** cars.
We can have fun with the cars.

10 little **white** cars.

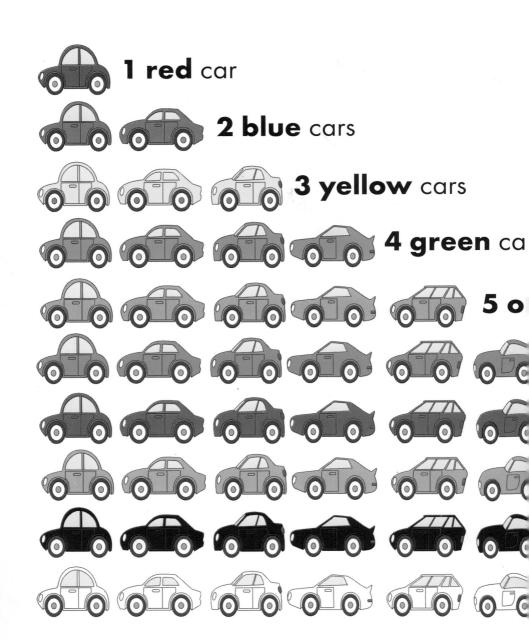

1 red car

2 blue cars

3 yellow cars

4 green ca

5 o

ge cars

brown cars

 **7 purple** cars

 **8 pink** cars

 **9 black** cars

 **10 white** cars

Wow!
Look at this.
So many cars.
So many, many cars.

Here you are with me.
And here I am with you.
What fun.
What fun, dear dragon.

READING REINFORCEMENT

The following activities support the findings of the National Reading Panel that determined the most effective components for reading instruction are: Phonemic Awareness, Phonics, Vocabulary, Fluency, and Text Comprehension.

Phonemic Awareness: The /ar/ sound

Sound Substitution: Say each of the following words to your child and ask your child to tell you which two words rhyme:

park, dark, pack	jar, jam, far	yam, yarn, barn
shark, shack, bark	cage, barge, large	harp, tap, tarp
part, mart, mat	had, card, hard	

Phonics: /ar/ Phonograms

1. Explain to your child that sometimes, the letter **r** after a vowel changes the sound of the vowel (for example, can/car).

2. Fold a piece of paper in half the long way twice.

3. Draw a line down the folds to divide the paper into four parts.

4. Write the phonograms **-ar**, **-ard**, **-arm**, and **-art** in separate columns at the top of the page.

5. Write the following words on separate (small) pieces of paper or index cards:

car	cart	card	farm	far
part	dart	star	tart	yard
harm	smart	lard	arm	tar
charm	jar	hard	chart	bar

6. Have your child underline the phonogram in each word.

Vocabulary: Color Words

1. Write the following words on separate pieces of paper or index cards:

black   blue   brown   green   orange

pink   purple   red   white   yellow

2. Read each word to your child and ask your child to repeat it.

3. Ask your child to trace over the letters with crayon or marker, using the corresponding color (you might suggest that your child revisit the book for help).

4. Mix the words up. Point to a word and ask your child to read it. Provide clues if your child needs them. For example:

This is the color of pumpkins. (orange)

Grass is this color in spring. (green)

Panda bears and zebras are these two colors. (black and white)

Fluency: Echo Reading

1. Reread the story to your child at least two more times while your child tracks the print by running a finger under the words as they are read. Ask your child to read the words he or she knows with you.

2. Reread the story, stopping after each sentence or page to allow your child to read (echo) what you have read. Repeat echo reading and let your child take the lead.

Text Comprehension: Discussion Time

1. Ask your child to retell the sequence of events in the story.

2. To check comprehension, ask your child the following questions:

- How many pink cars does the boy have?
- What happened to the orange cars?
- What color do the boy and his mother both like?
- What is your favorite color? Why?

WORD LIST

Dear Dragon's Colors 1,2,3 uses the **56 pre-primer vocabulary words listed below**. This list can be used to practice reading the words that appear in the text. You may wish to write the words on index cards and use them to help your child build automatic word recognition. Regular practice with these words will enhance your child's fluency in reading connected text.

a	fun	look	red	wow
am				
and	go	make	so	yellow
are	good	many		you
at	green	me	the	
		Mother	them	
black	have		they	
blue	here	not	this	
brown	how		to	
		oh	too	
can	I	orange		
car(s)	in	out	up	
come	is			
	it	pink	we	
dear		play	what	
down	like(s)	pretty	white	
dragon	little	purple	with	

ABOUT THE AUTHOR Margaret Hillert has written over 80 books for children who are just learning to read. Her books have been translated into many different languages and over a million children throughout the world have read her books. She first started writing poetry as a child and has continued to write for children and adults throughout her life. A first grade teacher for 34 years, Margaret is now retired from teaching and lives in Michigan where she likes to write, take walks in the morning, and care for her three cats.

Photograph by Glenna Washburn

ABOUT THE ADVISER Shannon Cannon contributed the activities pages that appear in this book. Shannon serves as a literacy consultant and provides staff development to help improve reading instruction. She is a frequent presenter at educational conferences and workshops. Prior to this she worked as an elementary school teacher and as president of a curriculum publishing company.